James Rockcliffe

The Camp of the Hallamshires

And other Poems

James Rockcliffe

The Camp of the Hallamshires
And other Poems

ISBN/EAN: 9783744764827

Printed in Europe, USA, Canada, Australia, Japan

Cover: Foto ©Andreas Hilbeck / pixelio.de

More available books at **www.hansebooks.com**

THE

Camp of the Hallamshires,

AND OTHER

POEMS.

BY

JAMES ROCKCLIFFE.

SHEFFIELD:
PAWSON AND BRAILSFORD, PRINTERS, HIGH-STREET.
1865.

TO THE

Right Hon. Lord Wharncliffe,

LIEUTENANT-COLONEL OF THE HALLAMSHIRE RIFLE
VOLUNTEERS,

This Volume

IS, BY SPECIAL PERMISSION, RESPECTFULLY DEDICATED

BY ONE

WHO, AS A VOLUNTEER, IS PROUD TO BELONG TO THE CORPS,

AND

WILL EVER ACKNOWLEDGE HIS LORDSHIP'S KINDNESS

BY

ENDEAVOURING TO DESERVE IT.

PREFACE.

Soon after returning from Ringstone Hill encampment, the Author formed the intention, in accordance with the expressed wish of several members of the corps, of describing the scene of so much enjoyment, in prose, which he believes would have been the best medium for doing so. Circumstances, however, have since suggested the publication of poems, among which " The Camp" has taken its chance in that form,

Our friends must not suppose that, if we had our fun, we had not our work also, for by judiciously combining both, we contrived to render it an event never to be forgotten in our volunteering existence. We can only refer to the universal regard—of which we have had ample proofs—in which the corps was held by the inhabitants of the surrounding districts, and we can only hope that succeeding encampments may be as successful, and yield as much general satisfaction.

A great number of very enjoyable events may, very probably, have been omitted, but to indulge in a complete description would have occupied a book of similar size to the present one, and it would hardly be possible for all of them to have come under the notice of one individual.

It has been a generally cherished opinion, but one which is fast disappearing with other vulgar prejudices, that the poetical temperament is incompatible with the more practical and business-like occupations of every-day life, but a reference to examples like Telford, the great engineer, and the present illustrious Earl of Derby, and many other eminent men, is a sufficient reply to such ill-conceived opinions. The Author, then, can only launch his little book, trusting it will have a fair trial in the hands of an impartial public, who must do him the justice to remember that " The Camp" poem is the result of five weeks' study only. All jocular allusions must be received in the genial spirit they are intended.

1st January, 1865.   J. R.

The Camp of the Hallamshires.

— ⊖ —

'Twas in the year **One-eight-six**-four,
  On RINGSTONE HILL did lay
A brave and dashing **rifle corps,**
  In proud and bold array !

So big drums beat, and colours **stream'd**
  And flaunted in the air ;
Oh, little had the country dream'd
  What stirrings would be there !

When scarlet coats make manly hearts
  Beat 'neath them,—girls, beware—
For bayonets and Cupid's darts
  Are side by **side, I** swear !

On every point a poison **lies**—
  Delicious poison, **too ;**
And quickly thro' the frame it **flies,**
  And **marks** " red, white, and blue."

Then let us here recount **the** fame
  Of our brave **Rifle Corps,**
That earned itself a glorious name
  In One-eight-and-six-four !

'Tis night !

Struggling, jumbling,

Grumbling, fumbling,

Three figures emerge from the dark—

And stumbling about,

With a stifled shout,

They seem as if missing their mark !

Lo ! a boy, on the top of a mare rather thin—
On which to be outside would hurt you, but in
There wouldn't be room for a good feed of corn,
And it seem'd a great wonder how Lubin was borne.
To decide, 'twould seem to require some " nous,"
'Tween the ridge of a horse and the ridge of a house.

But, thro' mire and mud,

With a slip and " thud,"

These three forms quiver and quaver about,

And, as darker it grows,

Each one puffs and blows,

Gets thirsty, for " wayside inns" looks sadly out ;

And as the dark shroud

Of o'erhanging cloud

Seems to wrap the night-cloak over all,

They hurry along,

As the well-plied thong

Makes the old mare wish hard for her stall.

What is that ?—what is that ?

'Tis a bright face, and fat,

And good-tempered, looks out at the door ;

In the ruddy glow
Of the fire, the flow
Of good-humour'd laughter lets us know
That this is the inn—nor poor
Is the entertainment for man and beast—
And, to tell all the truth, and to say the least,
'Tis hard sometimes to tell,
Without one knows well,
Which is the man, and which is the beast !

" Halt ! " is the word, and the figures appear,
As they hasten to dash the white froth from their beer;
Thus as they pass in—like Banquo's ancestral
And long line of Kings—these parties conquestral
Glide onward in dignity into the kitchen
Of the " Old Crown" at Houghton, a great Exhibition !
Let us describe this trio queer who thus disturb the night,
As now they come within the glow of ruddy fire-light.
The taller traveller sits him down, and with important
    mien
He looks around as tho' to see them all, and to be seen ;
In scarlet is he well arrayed, with bayonet, belt, and pouch,
And as the little country boys in eager wonder crouch
Around, he calls for nut-brown ale to soothe his
    thirsty frame.
His voice is high, his nod immense, for many a
    buxom dame
In his " mind's eye" already he hath wooed, and boldly
    won ;
For, tho' in No. 2 he is, he thinks of No. One.

The other **hath** a sober look,
   And nice white choker on ;
And, could we write another book,
   His praise might still **go on.**
He sits him down **right cosily**
   Upon an easy chair,
And seems in **peace** reposily
   To bid " Good-bye" **to** care.
He says nice quiet things—" Just so,"
   " I see," and " Yes," and " Well ! "
" I never ! " " Did you, really ! " " Oh ! "
   " Of course," and rings the bell.

The youth, well fagged and sleepy, blows
A loud " last post—er" thro' his nose,
And soft dreams **through his rough head** creep.
As on a bench he drops asleep.
Who **would not envy that poor boy,**
Whose slumber is a dream of joy ?

Rise up, rise up, **my** merry, merry souls,
   The tide is flowing strong,
Of blinks and winks **from** faces red,
By curiosity well fed—
   A stout and sturdy throng ;
Of farmers who the festive e'en
   Spin out with tale and song.
Rise up, rise up, for hither rolls
   The tide, nor can we stay
These mighty bodies, jolly souls—

Oh, what a long, long way
A drop of "short" will go, applied but in a know-
    ing way !

Slyly and slowly, then, one by one,
    The natives come gliding in—
Uncle and nephew, and father and son,
    With their stout, their beer, and their gin.
Cautiously spread they around and sip,
And as their "physogs" they busily dip
Into " each cup and into each can,"
They cannily survey the soldier-man—
Who, in his hilarity, sings 'em a song,
(Whether in right or whether in wrong.)
The music he opens with rustyish key,
For of great and good music a judge isn't he—
    So he doesn't detain 'em long.

" Yes, let me like a soldier fall ! "
And there breaks down the midnight bawl.
The speech that follows song so queer
Is wondrous funny, and doth cheer ;
And now into the night so drear
The travellers are a-foot again.
And soon the farm they gladly gain,
Where hissing ham from browning coals
Soon lies upon their plates in shoals.
The youthful Lubin puts his head
Beneath the grate, and dreams it's bread ;
And, as the ham's choice drops do trickle off,
His cakey head it makes a pickle of!

Slowly and sadly the trav'llers rise
  At five in the morn ;
And as each rubs his heavy and obstinate eyes
  With feelings forlorn,
The neighing of horses, the bleating of cows,
And all such like agricultural rows
      Make 'em imagine
      They must have been cadging,
And they are the calves getting mix'd with the cows !

The fresh morning's breath is along the brown heather,
And couples are hast'ning to labour together ;
The bright blue is stretching o'er mountain and vale,
And each rosy-cheek'd lass is abroad with her pail.
Young foxhounds are bounding about in their glee,
O'er the broad country side, so fair, bonny, and free.
As the whip cracks, the teamster is rumbling along,
The old mare cocks her ears to the time-honoured song
That tells how poor Mary, the pride of the vale,
Died young, through hard drinking at very strong ale,
And the dead (in the spirit) doth nightly appear
To her " lovier," in white, in the froth on his beer !
So when he's been eating at things indigestible
Her horrible figure is quite incontestible !
Then, whistling and singing, light hearts onward go,
To the tune of " Gee, Dobbin, gee up, and gee whoa ! "

In silence, without beat of drum,
In camping life, a few will come

To pitch the tents, and clear the way,
A " party " called " fatigue," they say,
That though there were indeed but few
To do the work of scores, they knew,
And bent their bodies to the task,
Nor would the aid of others ask.
Their leader stripped him to the sleeve,
And would his men by turns relieve ;
Proving himself no slothful lurker,
But on the contrary a worker.
And many a joke, and laugh, and song
Cheered well the workers' hearts along ;
And when the day's hard work was done
In social happiness each one
Would sit him down beneath the tree
So famous for its minstrelsie !
By able sergeants aided well—
Men who in strong-armed citadel
Had brav'd the foe, and in the field
Forced him, unwillingly, to yield !

Without condescension,
We may as well mention
Without meaning harm,
In that fine old farm
Homestead on the hill
There are eyes that kill
Without using skill ;
For Nature, sweet Nature, gives grace to the charms
Of those fair young ladies

To whom **praise best paid is**
In saying they **stuck to** our colours and **us,**
Without any nonsense, without any fuss,
Bless'd our hearts, and bade Providence prosper our
arms !

Tho tents arise in seven white rows,
   And dotted o'er the ground,
As each its welcome outline **shows**
Each eye with hopeful ardour glows,
   And looks in triumph round !
In pride **we** contemplate the scene,
   Sore back **and** blister'd hand
Proclaim what hard-worked boys we've **been,**
What labour done, what service seen,
   And how adorned the land !

And when the tents we have done pitching
We'll sit and sing in that old kitchen,
Where once in " ingle-nook " lay chirping
The cricket that had welcomed Turpin !

Of things **most** unromantic,
And calculated **to drive frantic,**
   Is digging **a hole**
   For a pole ;
But there's fun in the thought
That a " verdant " you've caught
   With a tale
   That turns pale

The "greenhorn" who opens his mouth very wide,
   As if there were room
   The pole to entomb,
The clock that goes on it, and "navvies" beside !
  Alas ! the Barkshi–aw Volunte–aw ;
  When he had asked—" Pray, what is he–aw ?'
    With grief in face,
    And solemn grace
  We said :—" The grave in which we bury
   " The dead when slain in action,
   " For their friends' satisfaction !"—
  He said :—" Quite charming, ve-wy !"
   And so, with fun to wile the day,
   The day and night soon passed away.

Hark, hark, 'tis the tramp and the sound that we love,
 So merrily sounding near,
As each echo awakes in the hills far above,
 'Tis the music " we love to hear."
   With bugle and drum
   The red lines come,
 And the foremost ranks appear !
   Rushing and squeezing,
   Crushing and wheezing,
All the old men in the country are here ;
   And the old scent of battle
   Comes fresh with the rattle
Of arms, and their legs run quicker and quicker,
And shrivelly muscle grows thicker and thicker,
   As the old women patter

And clatter **and chatter,**
With their whims and their oddities, fancies **and** graces,
Glad to see their old men with those bright smiling faces,
That are usually kept for their fireside places !

See, where approach, with quicken'd tread,—
The gallant major at their head,
As country folk around them crowd,—
The dusty troops so wondrous **proud ;**
And though their fame has oft been told,
We may describe these captains bold,
As Homer, Virgil, and the rest of 'em
Had to describe the very best of 'em.

First, **our Commander, on whose face**
Sits serious **thought** with manly grace ;
His word is law, his heart and soul
Are in the rifle muster-roll ;
And **next, our** Adjutant, whose calm
And staid demeanour gives a charm
To. all he says **or** does—a man
In battle, or the Christian van
Who would be foremost. Number " One "
Can boast a chief whose duty's done
Correctly, so precise **of tread,**
So clear in tone, erect of head,
That all who see him wish to **be**
Tho captain of a company !
With modest step and anxious eye
The chief of " Number Two " goes by ;

He leads a small but glorious band,
Who doubtless could a host withstand ;
Their hearts with valour would be fired
Nor end in smoke, were they required !
Then " Three " and " Four," no captain comes,
Nor marches to our martial drums ;
The world of commerce where he reigns
Demands him, there to handle reins
That, guided by his able hand,
Hold the vast Atlas at command !
Then " Five " hath one for choral power
Well famed, when in a peaceful hour,
And subalterns as famous, all
We can with pride superiors call.
Who ably aid their chiefs, and strive
To cheer us on that we may thrive.
See " Number Six"—with form agile
Their warrior springs upon the heel,
And willing boys his presence feel ;
Athletic deeds of high renown
Have given him long the " laurel crown."
So keen of eye, compact of limb,
Aspiring youths may envy him.
And last, not least, amid the din
Comes the smart dash of discipline,
As " Number Seven" upon the plain
Has mustered well and not in vain—
So, flashing back each wand'ring ray,
Their gallant chieftain leads the way ;
His gay lieutenant, following, shows

The path where heartfelt merit glows
In hearts enshrined that serve him well,
And best in deeds affections tell.*
We miss our noble Colonel ; he
Would have encamped most happily.
Affairs of State his presence claim ;—
We can but love his honoured fame,
And have him with us but in name.

As when the war-horse scents afar
The grim and gory field of war,
And pricks his ears at welcome sounds—
At bugle-blast his heart rebounds—
He proudly stands to view the host,
In meditation seems quite lost—
E'en so our veteran sees a gleam
From one bright star in glory's **dream,**
His life 'neath India's sun yet gives
In spirit, and for glory lives.
And as we thus recount, 'tis fair
We yield our praise to his confrère ;
Our kind and willing soldier dear
Must ever be our **" Musketeer."**
The strains of martial music **sweep**
The echoes far and wide, in **deep**
And varied tone—for notes are there
Produced by those we ill can spare,
Who soon, alas ! in death shall rest,
Eternal slumber with the blest !

---

* The Lieutenant alluded to was presented with a valuable
sword by " No. Seven" Company, in Camp, on August 9, 1864.

" Halt ! Lodge arms ! " they soon obey.
" Quick, strew your beds ;" all hands away.
The shades of eve are o'er the plain,
And " last posts" first night's camp proclaim.

To bed, to bed,
Each weary head.
See, glimmering tents, like so many lanterns,
With a buzz like big bees
Give in roots of trees ;
While a slight breeze is stirring that hardly a fan turns.
Whilst some darkly are courting
Old Murphy in slumber ;
And these are by many long
Odds the least number.
Whilst sleep may forsake
Eyes that cannot partake
Of it, whilst fellows make
Rows like " Christians awake,"
And tumble about on their beds just like lumber.

Lo ! shivering forms in silence creep,
Condemned to hear the others sleep ;
For HEARING is the truest sense
In which to take a snore immense—
Which, if the noses to the sound
At all proportion, I'll be bound
It would be hard to find the tents
To cover some such ornaments.
Themes these for physiologists,

Phrenolo—— no, nosologists.
Two hither come, well tired and worn,
For guard at night and drill at morn
Hath bronzed their brows and scaled their hands,
And made their arms like iron **bands.**
We'll listen as they sit and chew
Reflection's cud amid the dew,
As herald morn precedes the day,
In a pale grey and foggy way :—

" What is it chills thy marrow so,
   And makes thy face look old ?
Why dost thou contemplative grow,
   And tremble with the cold ?

" **What is** it pinches up thy face,
   And **makes** thy voice so thin—
Since thine is **not a woful case**
   Of sick, or short of tin ?"

" **I ne'er was** out so late before,
   But snug with my dear wife,
I did escape affliction sore—
   She solaceth my life."

" I've seen queer things **the** nights that I
   Have been a sentry here,
Such sights, **such sounds** I've heard, for lie
   I dare not, for I fear !

" Just now I heard some breathing, deep,
    And sonorously slow ;
Strange beings horrid vigils keep,
    And seem to groan below.

" By yon end tent I stumbled o'er
    A dusky form supine,
 ' Queer whiskey ! ' murmured he, and ' Pour
    On, on ; there's nowt like wine ! '

" And then he fell a-grumbling, so—
    As if internal pain
    Had somewhat quenched the happy glo-
    Rious vintage of Champagne !

" Two larkish youths, in merry vein,
    Came ' tripping o'er the lea,'
And, jumping on our prostrate swain,
    Seemed glorying in the spree !

" A dreadful noise quick rose within,
    And elf-like sounds were heard,
Then snoring did at once begin,
    As if naught had occurred !

" Close by, two rogues, right full of fun,
    Would then by turns recite,
Both blest with lungs, and there is one
    In love tales takes delight.

" And while the rest are snug at rest,
　　This pious pair will kick
Each other out—as if unloosed
　　Asylum lunatic !

" Then doth some poor, exhausted wretch
　　Sink down 'neath Nature's laws,
Just forty winks in vain to catch,
　　'Mid laughter and applause.

" Ye gods, ye gods, when warriors fall
　　Subdued by potent nectar,
'Tis time, indeed, " Police" to call,
　　Or ' Nuisances' Inspector ! '

" **There is one** pensive youth whose deep
　　Bassoon-like tones, when **heard,**
Seem rumbling where the dismals sleep,
　　In twelve inch pipe interred !

" He hath a tall-complexioned face,
　　With bumps of wisdom big,
On well-proportion'd knowledge case
　　That's far from ' infra dig.'

" He **can write** well, and they who can't
　　May be satirical ;
But if 'tis doubted, see the Pant-
　　Omimic miracle !

" As he is young and in his prime,
    We hope he'll oft be here,
And with well-written pantomime
    Turn up trump ev'ry year.

" Another night the camp awoke—
    For, struggling with the guard,
A burly farmer licence took,
    And trampled on our sward.

" The ' lamb' who soon can soothe alarms
    Is chubby, round, and tall ;
He took him kindly in his arms,
    But heavy let him fall.

" The bulky Joskin's fall was such
    Would come from bullock's blow—
Poor Joskin got a drop too much,
    And scorned a second ' go.'

" Sometimes a sound comes sharp upon
    The quiet, balmy air—
Hark ! 'tis ' Another bottle, John ! '
    'Tis gay ' Sir Mousquetaire.'

" Oh ! could'st thou see him in the dance,
    Or nimbly thread the maze—
He can a hornpipe neatly prance,
    With wondrous steps amaze!

B

" He plants his pins with charming grace,
    And, with unerring aim,
  He drops upon **a** soft green place,
    And bounces up **again.**

" **I** do not feel so chilly now—
    I'm warming with my tale ;
  Yet I must let thee hear, **I trow,**
    About the fearful gale.

" **When** sleep **was** going gently on
    One night, a doleful cry
Was heard—the flags of (Number One)
    Distress were flapping by.

" For, **oh ! great guns the** fierce wind blew,
    And hard the canvas strain'd,
So quickly stalwart tent-pegs drew,—
    While some **affirm** it rained.

" The **victims** plunged, and tugged, and ran,
    As the wild **storm** passed o'er ;
They blessed themselves, and to a man
    Said **cursory** things, and swore !

" But if it rained, 'twixt **you and** me,
    It was such ' heavy wet',
Tents couldn't **stand**—the cham-pag-ne
    I never shall forget.

" To tell the truth, I had a taste—
    I found it in my hand—
  I could not—would you?—let it waste,
    'Twould spoil to let it stand.

" But what we wonder'd most at was,
    How one tent could so roll,
  And not the next—it was because
    It had an extra pole !

" The wind pass'd on—the sky went bright,
    Sky-high—it all passed o'er ;
  And thus a rather active night
    Was passed by all the corps,

" In which our splendid pioneers
    Played well their useful part ;
  Their talent usually appears
    Most in the building art.

" For they are perfect ' Kings of spades,'
    Which they can wield so well ;
  And choice retreats in sylvan glades
    Can best their prowess tell.

" A few odd things, when I reflect,
    Have here omitted been,
  And I can just now recollect,
    More frolics to have seen.

" Some roguish fellow, for a lark,
　　Had found some wine—to share **it**
He much desired—the wicked spark
　　Had seized a dose of claret !

" But, Oh ! the mouth he pulled—how queer ;
　　'Twas vinegar, he swore ;
His mouth was pulled from ear to ear,
　　" Which was not so before."

" 'Twould seem an erring soul to warn,
　　(If the cap fits, who'll wear it ?)
The sweets at night, the sours at morn ;
　　He could but grin and bear it.

" A blue policeman came one night,
　　And so was challenged flat ;
He cried, ' I'm Double **X.'** ' All right—
　　You'll pass the lines with that ! '

" Did'st ever see, at break of day,
　　The famous bucket-trick,
And Reuben **in a** pleasant way
　　The well-filled bucket kick ?

" He **hath a rival,** who hath fame
　　Nearly as great as he ;
But when he **tried to do** the same
　　It fell, unhappily.

" Right on the summit of his crown
    It fell—well whacked and sore,
He was declared a clean break-down,
    For he was cracked before.

" One doth our quiet slumbers mock
    With chanticleering—so,
As of the walk he can't be cock,
    He doth a sorry crow!

He stops—the spot whereon he stood
    He standeth not—for whack,
He's down a rabbit-hole, you should
    Have heard his spinal crack !

He pulls a melancholy face,
    But then, with effort quick
He doth the lucky chance embrace—
    Joke hypochondri—ick !

" All's square, as yet," he roundly swears,
    " Tho' nicked in by these furrows,
I can't be canvass in, for there's
    No standing for the burrows !"

" But we must part, I hear the crow
    Of rural chanticleer.
Again we'll meet, before we go
    To Sheffield." " I'll be here."

We must astir—the game is up, and crowds upon us
come.
Would'st know the cause ? A fearful deed will sure
this day be done ;
A Volunteer hath broken laws of discipline, they say,
And will be hanged up by the neck in an ignoble way.

Besides, the French are on the coast, by Grimsby, and
they cry
The Gallic watchword lustily, are " coming by-and-bye."
The country folk have watched all night till early
break of day
For foes of grim and grisly mien, in horrible array.

Jack hath told Bob, and Bob to Dick hath wagged his
turnip head ;
Hath jumped up in his sleep, and heard the dismal ogre's
tread ;
Hath tried his rusty helmet on, and girded well his flail,
And filled his leathern bottle full of valour-giving ale.

But hapless wag, could he be found who'd spread the
wicked tale,
With serious face had turned the tap-room customers
all pale,
He would the weight of some huge fist upon his carcass
feel,
Could some unlucky circumstance his presence here
reveal.

Away he slinks, **and wisely** thinks, to keep well out of
  sight,
Is much the best, and have a rest, be in concealment
  quite.
" Potato-drill " he loves, **for** there he gets out **of all**
  share in
Hard work, and with the girls he feels much more at
  home in paring.

When evening comes he hies him up into the mystic **tree,**
Whose glory we **have** sung before **as** famed for **min**-
  strelsie ;
And there, with jovials **all around,** he pipes the daylight
  out—
Whilst listening folk **in little groups** encircle them about.

Song—" The Bees."
Air—" Guy Fawkes."

How doth the little buzzy bee improve each shining hour,
And gather honey **as he** flies o'er ev'ry tempting flower ;
His human prototype **I mean, who,** as through life **he**
  goes, sirs,
Sucks knowledge from each little **bud that on life's big**
  tree grows, sirs.
Buzz, buzz, buzz !
Ri fol deriddy-iddy—buzz, buzz, buzz !

NOTE.—*This elegant and expressive chorus **must be repeated**
  carefully.*

How doth he then, throughout his **life, some sound ex-**
    perience gather ;
But this, like garden honey culled, depends on Fortune's
    weather.
So in the sunshine of the week he gathers o'er and o'er,
    sirs,
Against the jolly night in camp, where he unpacks his
    store, sirs.
Buzz, buzz, buzz, &c.

How like, then, to the buzzy bee, wo husband up each
    treasure
Of wit or sparkling anecdote, of song in sprightly mea-
    sure,
And chink **the** glass of fellowship, of love from man to
    man, sirs—
When heart and hand are pledged in **one, what** better
    social band, sirs ?
Buzz, buzz, buzz, &c.

And when **we**'ve grown careworn and grey, we'll sit out-
    side the hive, sirs ;
Be glad **to see** the young folks' **joy,** and help 'em all **to**
    thrive, sirs.
We'll none of us feel worse **for that, for we** shall do to
    them, sirs,
What we would they should do to us, and so you'll say
    Amen, sirs.
Buzz, buzz, buzz, &c,

Moral.

So, while we sit and take our case, we'll care not for
    outsiders,
Who always claim the sov'reign right of critics or de-
    riders.
We'll do as friendship doth inspire, whatever others say,
    sirs—
For every " cat will have his mew," each " dog will have
    his day," sirs.

Buzz, buzz, buzz, &c,

Then loud applause succeeds—all give chorus to the strain,
And oft the singer's called upon to give it once again.
But time wears on, and others, blest with heart and
    voice to sing,
To tune a stave, attention crave, and make the welkin ring!

Song—" The Hallamshire Rifles." *
Air—" Lieutenant Luff."

The founder of the Sheffield corps
    Make known to foe and friend,
And do not underrate his pains—
    For he was Overend ;
'Twas when of hostile foes the land
    Was filled with dire alarms,
And many a British matron held
    Light infantry in arms,
Fol de rol, &c.

* Sung and contributed by Corporal W. E. Bullmore, of
No. 2 Company, H.R.V.

The threats which o'er the ocean came
  Were not to be endured,
And being open to the sea,
  We were not well insured.
So hoary age and fair-haired youth
  Soon formed a gallant band—
Boys left their mothers' apron strings
  For love of fatherland.
          Fol de rol, &c.

Among the host which then arose
  Up sprang the Sheffield corps,
And every member scorns to own
  That drill was o'er a bore.
Mechanics learn to work by files ;
  And, if I don't mistake,
Our shopkeepers and business **men**
  Can heavy charges **make.**
          Fol **de rol, &c.**

Our wealthy men drill side by side
  With those who are in need—
The pride of those who'd scorn our ranks
  Is very rank indeed.
Now I must ask that at my lines,
  You will not jeer and scoff;
And, having finished up my song,
  Why, now I will " break **off.**"
          Fol de rol, &c.

THE SABBATH.

How peaceful is the calm,
　　As Houghton's village bell
　　To pious folk doth tell
　　　The hour of prayer !
How soothing is the balm,
And nature seems refreshed, as yon bright sun
Comes forth with cheering rays, that deeds begun
　　　In holy thought may give
　　　Sweet solace while we live,
　　　And bless us There !

How gentle is the power
　　Of that subdued appeal,
　　As formed in square we kneel
　　　Before high Heaven !
How solemn is the hour !
The clash of arms is hushed, and all is still,
Save when the songs of praise the courtyard fill !*
　　　Each reverently bows—
　　　Heard are his earnest vows—
　　　And he's forgiven !

* The court-yard alluded to is that of the Old Hall, at
Houghton, which is a fine architectural specimen of the
olden time, and of great historical interest.

NIGHT, 8TH AUGUST, 1864.

A BLAZE ! A BLAZE !
 A blaze of light,
'Mid the wild gaze
 Of many a wight !

Now gleams of red light broadly thrown
Along the country, red sparks grown
To vivid flame, then quickly rise,
And shoot across toward the skies ;
Thus as the coming breezes fan
The flapping flame from man to man,
As round they stand, in forks and sheets
The red fire comes, the heather heats,
And dusky stifling vapour flies
With crackling sound where pussy lies,
Who bounds away, and with a cry
Of terror, dashes swiftly by.
 Thick wreaths of smoke
From lambent fire now roll along,
 The slumber broke
Of many a rustic ; then the song
 Peals upward o'er the echoing hills,
 And every bird with wonder fills,
  Who rushing down,
  The flame surround,
And shouts with jocund laughter sorrow kills

  Right round they go,
  With heel and toe,

The girls and boys—
No sad alloys
Are here to check unbidden joy ;
Both song and dance
The joy enhance,
And lasses, rosy-cheeked and coy,
Smile sweetest approbation,
And all their gentle arts employ,
Without their affectation.

With baton huge and measured sweep,
A lusty wag the time doth keep,
And with a most portentous swing
Proclaims himself the great "Fire-king,"
Who magic wand wields single-handed.
Each burning brand
He can command,
For he's good-sorted, and well brandied !

Thus happy hours speed on,
And when the folk have gone,
Some wand'ring youth, whose leave has long expired,
Upon his hands and knees,
Afraid to cough or sneeze,
Anxious to reach the tent he's long desired,
Doth creep ; the sentry spies
His gliding form, and cries :
"Who goes there?" "Friend !" " Stand, friend,
advance and give
The counter-pane. Oh ! no—that's wrong, yes, as
I live,

It's counter*mand* :
Then you, sir, stand."
" **I** can't, so that's straight tip superlative !
I'm fond of nice old trees, **and** been
To ' Well-bred Oak.' " **Says** sentry,
" You'**re** ' up a tree,' I'm not so green,
A bad-bred hoax—no entry !"

The dying embers crackle, burn
A moment, then go out in turn ;
The smoke has clear'd away, and all
The village cocks a-sleeping fall ;
The goose's last portentous cackle
Has silenced with the ember's crackle ;
The pig, on whose huge brawny **sides**
The farmer prides himself, now hides
Himself in **straw, a** loving union,
But not **a very sweet communion !**
For **never** had **these** quadrupeds
Been roused before so from their beds ;
That morning e'en 'twas said the cock
Declin'd to crow till eight o'clock,
And said, These troops must very soon retreat,
Or I for one shall never make ends meet.

At five the bugle sounds " all **up**"
The volunteers,—but down, not **up**
Are they,—the **rain too, all the** camp
Is murky, gloomy, vapoury, damp ;
Thus, **heat within, and wet** without,
Each tent has quite a cloud about

Of steam ; and as the pelting rain
Comes down and doth the canvas strain,
Full many a strain within is heard,
And each one singing " like a bird."

" **The show,** the show !
Walk up, **walk up here,** just a-going to begin :
Big-'uns and little-'uns, just step a minute in,
This is the real original and only show in the fair !
Little boys with dirty noses, keep off the steps, take care!
Ehey ! **Ehey ! !** Ehey ! ! !"

" This is the wild Horum-Borum-Squeak from Timbuctoo,
For size, make, and shape, for height and breadth and **hue,**
There's nothing like **him here** or there, **or anywhere** in
creation,
And, as the Yankies say, we can with truth **that** he'll
lick tarnation.
Ehey ! Ehey ! ! Ehey ! ! ! Ehey ! ! ! !"

" Just stir him **up,"** and then a din with cornet, fife,
and drum,
Enough to thump off all our ears, **and kill Horum-Borum ;**
The crowd soon gather round and **stare, and so seem
every** one
Determined to have **fun** or "nowt," the whole " hog
or none."

" **Now then,** now then, we've no connection with the
concern on the opposite side of the way ;

You don't see a pig in his wild, uncultivated **state, and**
  with a " chevaux-de-frise" **back** every day ;
Old folks, young folks, full price after dinner—those **who**
  can't get any, half the usual figure ;
Be it known (*gong !*) to all men, **that we** charge an extra
  copper for every size bigger.
" Ehey, ehey, ehey," up goes the hedgehog in the air
  and showman's hat goes quickly down,
Over his eyes, and he looks about in consternation **over**
  the shattered crown ;
A drumstick thus has closed the show, and **then the**
  news has quickly spread
That cold beef (and pickles !) are waiting, and poor
  Horum-borum's dead !

THE REVIEW **AND** RETURN.

The glorious sun in his golden prime
  Tints blossom, leaf, and spray ;
For genial is meridian time
  Of the bright warm summer's **day ;**
And martial sounds now fill
  The air, and serried men
March in measured tread of battalion drill
  At Ringstone **once** again !

The pleasant sward hath a new green dress,
  'Tis glossy 'neath the feet

Of the volunteers as they onward press,
  At " **quick** march" gaily meet ;
And anxious eyes are bent
  Upon their proud array—
On the steady lines in that armament
  In scarlet and in grey !

[**General** salute—Present arms—Shoulder arms—Rear **rank,**
take close order—March !—Open column right in front—
Right about face—Right wheel—Quick march—Halt, front,
dress—Slope arms—The **battalion will march past** in
quick time—Quick march—Battalion, halt—Left wheel into
line—Quick march—Halt—Officers and colours will take
post in review order—Quick march—Officers and colours
will take post with **their** battalions—Quick march— Take
ground to the right in fours—Right, quick march—Halt—
Extend—Retire—Alarm—Close **on** supports—Prepare to
receive cavalry—Ready—Present :—]

  Then the volley's flash
  As the chargers dash
  In mimic fight,
  To left, to right ;
  Extend again
  The riflemen ;
  " Close on reserve,"
  Nor doubt or swerve ;
  Shoulder and stand,
  Await command ;
  The work is **done,**

c

Ay, work and fun ;
We're very sorry, every one!

[Column—Shoulder arms—Present—Advance in review order—
March!]

Thus ends our Ringstone Hill review,
Our jollity and glory too ;
The crowds still linger on our track,
Ask often, will we soon come back ?
We wring their hands and make reply,
As best we can,—yes, bye and bye!

Farewell, then, to dear RINGSTONE HILL,
    Where oft, in early morn,
Bold sportsmen panting Reynard kill,
    And hunt with hound and horn ;
We leave it to the silent calm
    That o'er its wide domain
Awakes but to the shrill alarm
    Of " Tally-ho !"   Again
We say farewell to that fair spot,
    So sacred to the true
Faith politic without a blot,
    That willing thousands drew
To Ebenezer Elliott's verse,
    (He wrote it not in vain),
'Tis such that children may rehearse,—
    The " Corn-Law Rhymer's" strain.

HOMEWARD!

We come—we come—
With beat of drum,
And colours waving high ;
    At " Quick march, fours,"
    The red stream pours ;—*
A wild storm pelting by.

Then onward—on,
    We are upon
The road, and homeward hail,
    For colours none
    Have we that run,
We care not for the gale !

Whew ! 'tis a whirl
    Of wind—unfurl
Our banners to the blast ;
    Speed well along
    To farewell song,
We're homeward bound at last !

Hark ! 'tis a shout
    Comes ringing out,
Of crowds on our columns borne ;
    And grating sound
    Of cords unbound,
Of tents from moorings torn.

* We were overtaken by a violent storm.

Look—'tis the rout,
And wheel about,
Of that self-denying crew,
In queer attire,
'Mid mud and mire,
Self-sacrificing few!

We've done our best,
They'll do the rest,
Soon finish and have done;
Whate'er their tact,
It's quite a fact,
Their talent is to run!

Quick, 'tis the rush
Of crowds who flush
Our cheeks with healthy glow;
For 'tis not art
Here plays a part,
But Nature's honest flow!

Hark! 'tis the cheer
From village near,
As we pass around each **hill;**
The " good-bye" sung,
By old and young,
Crowding on each door-sill!

Young maidens **fair,**
Old men with hair

Snow-white, spread thinly o'er
   Their rev'rend pates,
   The scene elates,
Their war-days come once more !

   How many sighs
   And downcast eyes
We leave there behind us
   Will ne'er be known,
   But wiser grown,
Some hearts will be minus !

   We come, we come
   With beat of drum,
And heather branching high ;
   At " Quick march, fours,"
   The red stream pours:
Hill, field, and stream pass by !

   We come, we come
   With beat of drum—
Our homeward march is o'er ;
   To-night in town
   We sleep on down,
   Not heather brown—
And camp this year no more

In this short view of camping life
We have no need of pruning knife ;

The truth **is written, and the past**
Upon each page is freely cast,
To take its chance of praise or blame—
Whiche'er it is 'twill serve the same;
Our cause—whate'er revilers say—
Is country—kinsman; and the **day**
May be far distant when the blow
Can level'd be by foreign foe;
But far or near our hearts are free
And bold; in this we all agree,
War makes no soldier, but the chance
It gives him valour to enhance.
We are all soldiers, and the grave
That closes o'er each one hath brave
And noble dust within, the stuff
That e'er hath **made us** " **quantum suff**"
For any host who dare invade
Our country—then, lads, " **WHO'S AFRAID ?**"

Wharncliffe.

When Spring sweet bud and blossom gives,
And perfume in each flower lives,
As each with tiny insect life,
In sportive groups and colours rife,
We love the yielding turf to press
Amid the wild flowers' wilderness,
And hear the melody that chains
The willing heart with thrilling strains :
The song of birds that flutt'ring round
Enchant the listener with each sound ;
Or, when the Summer's sun is hot,
We strive to court the shaded grot,
Where, as the spreading boughs enlace,
Their glorious shelter we embrace ;
A lazy hum proclaims the bee
As idle as he well can be :
For one who is call'd " busy," surely
He earns his title most demurely.

When Winter with his icy hand
Spreads cold and pallor o'er the land,
And locks the rivers, lakes, and brooks
Up like iron-clasped books ;
The turf is crisp, the trees are bare,
And shiv'ring forms glide on with care
Along the crags so clear and gray,
And seem in fog to fade away.

Give me the Autumn time of year,
With sky and water bright and clear,

Both sparkling ; yet the air doth cheer
With balmy breath—how doubly dear
  Is sober Autumn-time !
At morn, when up the sportsman hies,
With dog and gun to covert flies,
He quickly game on wing espies :
The timid hare, too, faintly cries
  Her own death-note in time.
At mid-day when the gentle breeze
Plays with the gnarl'd and mighty trees,
The antler'd deer in terror flees
From shaggy bisons, whom he sees
  In munching silence feed ;
They take **no** heed of timid deer,
For none the bisons' wrath may fear,
Until their tails erect they rear,
And bark their compliments—too near,
  May then bo rash indeed.
Then o'er the beautiful **domain**
Wo seek not happiness in vain,
For from the hill-side to the plain
'Tis rich in tinted woods and grain,
  To cheer the wand'ring sight.
'Neath " Wharncliffe Crag" **is** wide **expanse,**
O'er which the clouds now seem **to** dance,
In days of yore, on plume and **lance,**
The mid-day sun would **gaily** glance,
  So beautiful and bright ;
Thus, in the valley stretching far,
The distant clang of deadly **war,**
With flashing helm and **scimitar,**

Would rouse the chivalry afar,
  And trumpet blast would ring
To horse, each knight and baron bold,
That could a lance or pennon hold,
On glory's page each name enroll'd—
Each deed of valour hath been told
  Of peasant, noble, king.
But peace now reigns supremely blest
O'er yon wide vale of blissful rest,
And on its fresh and verdant breast
Is many **a** love-tale now confest,
 And many a love-born sigh
Is breath'd **in** such sweet scenes, and by
Yon curling stream and wood close by,
We see young **lovers** wand'ring nigh,
And saying kind words pleasantly,
  And whispering " bye and bye."
· Away, then, o'er the craggy steep,
Down to the caverns dark and deep,
Where darksome reptiles croak and creep,
And small bright eyes around us peep,
  This is the Dragon's den !
" Dragon of Wantley," **famous he**
In legend, fable, history,
Who roam'd around so fearlessly,
  For he was monarch then !
Then " Wharncliffe," we must say adieu !
To heather, fox-glove, and blue-bell,
To wooded slope and verdant dell,
To glade and avenue, adieu !

Prologue,

*Spoken by the Author at the Sixth Private Amateur
Performance of the Liverpool Literary and Dramatic
Society, March 12th, 1858.*

As o'er Egyptian plains when sunrise broke,
From stone the rapturous strain of music **woke**,
And 'neath the magic of a spell-born power
Claim'd for itself the fable of an hour ;
So we, 'neath sunny smiles will strive to claim
" **A** local habitation and a name."
Or, as o'er spreading sands by ocean borne,
Now by the gentle wave, and now by storm,
Some little shell, unnoticed, may be **cast,**
Finding a quiet spot to lie at last ;
E'en so a passing thought may reach the heart,
And dwell there,—on the unconscious actor's part
Shedding a lustre that may last a day,
Then, like all things ephemeral, pass away !

Ye mimics, critics, poets, scribblers, wits,—
Each friend that **round us** in attention sits,—
Blunt the keen edge of satire in our cause,
We win bright laurels if with your applause !
Here, for an hour, forget your busy cares,
Loosen the mental weight that each one bears,
Some more,—some less,—in long and studious train,
Nor deem our aim to win you but in vain !

Ye who in commerce on the throng'd Exchange,
Your many schemes of wealthy venture range,
As your majestic ships o'er ocean bear
Proud news of England's glory everywhere,
Forget your speculations for awhile ;
We seek to draw a sympathetic smile ;
And whilst you leave behind the **busy** mart,
Will strive to captivate the indulgent **heart !**

Ye rising men, who pass **us** in review,
We needs must have **a passing word** with you ;
For we may show you here another **school,**
Where the old schoolmaster resumes **his rule ;**
Be not the lesson **to your hearts refused ;**
He'll teach—if you **don't** *learn* you'll be *amused.*

Ye ladies fair—(we must confess with **shame**
Our gallantry at fault—pray do not blame **!)**
We **claim your** sympathy, that still beguiles
The pain **of those who** seek to **win** your smiles.
Give us **a little place, however** fleeting,
In those **dear hearts**—(ah ! there are tell-tales beating !)
May they now throb **for us—ye happy** creatures—
Ye cannot guess **the** witchery of your **features !**
But gladly we receive, in fond subjection,
That which you well **can** spare—a faint reflection ;
And if **you** deem us **of our** theme uncertain,
Pray give the signal—and **down drops** the curtain.

Prologue,

To the " School for Scandal," played by the Liverpool Literary and Dramatic Society, in aid of the Bluecoat Hospital, at the Theatre Royal, Liverpool 23rd April, **1858.**

Upon the stage of life, from first to last,
Behold the shadows of an age gone past ;
Revealing days of our forefathers, when
An honest satire nerved the poet's pen,
Who pitied whilst he punished worthless **men.**
No cant defaced the genuine author's page,
As in these **days** of sychophantic rage
He strove to check ambition when **'twould aim**
(With truth and honour captive in the train)
To crush the world, **and trample on the** free,
And **in** oblivion blot out liberty !

Here let the curtain rise, and hence a ray
Throw light upon the moral of our play ;
And whilst we plead at Virtue's sacred shrine,
We feel her power, and own that power divine.
For doth not she in our affliction **breathe**
Kind words of solace ? O'er the dying wreathe
Hope's garland, bathed **in** pure and crystal springs,
Flowing **from whence** " the lark at heaven's gate sings ?"
Kind word or deed ne'er hesitates to give.
She lives to succour,—succours that we live,

Pours out a mine of wealth in mental lore,
Feeds with instruction those ne'er fed before,
With prosperous aim directing their career ;
As Charity we hail her presence here !
Bright messenger of love ! She fill'd the breast
Of that bold mariner, long since at rest,
Who, whilst his soul **was** warm'd **by** generous worth,
Prov'd that, howe'er obscure, unknown, his birth,
He could a temple rear with willing hand ;—
Such monuments *indeed* adorn our land.
His memory **lives** in every townsman's heart,
As one who played a more than glorious part ;
E'er faithful to one motto, borne by few,
" Stand *true* to *blue*, and it will prove *true blue !* "

Thus, while amidst the proud alarm of war,
That booms like distant thunder from afar,
While rebel nations tremble at our frown,
And firmly sits our blest Victoria's crown,
' Midst **all** the follies of a polish'd age
We read a wholesome lesson from the stage.
Tho' not a *new* one 'tis a *good* one,—fraught
With many a truth,—by school'd experience taught ;
And tho' that " School" be one of " Scandal," aid us
With all your hearts,—nor with slight faults upbraid us :
We claim no laurels : for this night's success
Is sacred to the young,—their hopes,—their happines !

Prologue,

SPOKEN BY MISS FORTESCUE

Before the Comedy of " Charles the 2nd," played by the
1st Cheshire Artillery Volunteers, on St. Valentine's
Day, 1862.

To-night we hold our Court, and thus the past
Pourtray upon the stage, our little " cast"
From folly strives a lesson good to give;
We live to learn, and learn that we may live,
Draw moral from our play, and by the stage
Reform the morals of each passing age.
Thus do we strive, in each eventful scene,
To captivate your hearts **with welcome theme.**
Though war, with loud artillery afar,
Bursts from a cloud in her triumphal car,
And **o'er** the ocean deep, with fiery breath,
Is heralding the pale advance of death,
Here peace yet reigns, in happy radiance—crown'd
With wreaths of glory where they most abound,
Where **art** and commerce, with unswerving **aim,**
Rise **'mid a** nation's prayers and glad acclaim ;—
Whence ships **convey** the wealth of every clime,
And prosperous enterprise denotes **the** time—
While a great Sovereign guides the helm of state,
For virtue makes our blest **Victoria great.**
And if a cloud of late hath overcast
Her happy royal home, 'tis of the past,

And may futurity's bright-lettered scroll
Bring blissful comfort to her wounded soul—
A nation's sympathies all-powerful prove
To soothe her, 'reft so early of her love.

But should the foe our much-loved homes invade,
Thus tempting death in hostile ranks arrayed,
Then may the lightning-flash of latent fires
That blazed within the bosoms of our sires
Burst forth more brightly 'midst Britannia's tears,
And all her sons prove faithful Volunteers !

Thus, while the world wags on, we pause awhile
To note the pleasant thought or transient smile :
And if to mimic life you'd fain attend
This evening, for a good and useful end,
We'll strive some share of your applause to gain,
And prove our *volunteering* not in vain.
In this night's short campaign we'll point the *gun*
Of sentiment and wit, of comic fun ;
So *fire*, and to the front in union steady
For your amusement or defence quite ready.
Thus to *enlist* your favours we combine,
Be one and all our loving *Valentine !*
And closing well King Cupid's holiday,
Each be a " Merry Monarch" in your way,
And heart and soul be with us in

THE PLAY.

Prologue,

Of the Liverpool Thespian Amateur Society, for a **Dramatic** *Performance in aid of the Lancashire Distress Fund, December* 18*th*, 1862.

How oft have minstrels gay, and poets, sung
Of festive pleasure, and their wild notes rung
Thro' History's page, of valorous deeds of might,
Of lady fair and brave mysterious knight ;
Of courtly dames, of glory—splendour—pride—
Of fearless warrior, and the timid bride !
And why ?   Because we those old legends love
Which can our wonder or amazement move !

But, in the quiet home of humble life,
Apart from **all** the great world's seething strife,
We see no bright romance, for thrifty care
Hath set its seal upon the poor man there !
—When prosperous times our favour'd country **bless,**
He toils—then homeward wanders to caress
All those to his rough, **honest** heart so dear ;—
Say, is the poet's theme not happier here **?**

But, now, alas !—where is the work to give
That our poor fellow-men may thrive and live ?
Those hearths which once in ruddy firelight shone
Are desolate—the merry faces gone,
Which then would crowd around them to relate

Their little joys, with youth and health elate !—
Now—crush'd and broken spirits drooping nigh,
Proclaim, **with** hollow visage **and** dimm'd **eye,**
The presence of pale want, that, brooding there,
Invites, 'mid desolation, dark despair !
They cannot beg, and **work** so long denied
Hath well **nigh crush'd** the workman's honest pride !
Weep, England, weep—for blood of brethren shed :
Weep—for our suffering thousands wanting bread !
Help, England, help—for all thy suffering band,
Who mourn, and starve **in** armies o'er the land :
And while, according it, *we'll* strive to charm
You, as you're casting in each mite of balm—
And as we strive our utmost to amuse,
To give us credit you will not refuse
For good intentions—think how blest **must be**
The pleasure that alleviates misery !

So now we'll pull the string ; the puppets pass
Before you **in** dame Nature's looking-glass :
An hour or two **will** doubtlessly proclaim
Our faults and failings : " TIME TRIES ALL" the same :
And if you hesitate in your applause,
" WHO SPEAKS FIRST"—let him not forget our cause—
Forget not in your flow of happiness
That you're relieving " Lancashire Distress !"

D

The Royal Wedding.*

WRITTEN 10TH MARCH, 1863.

CHARACTERS.

ALBION, CALEDONIA, ERIN, CAMBRIA, MERCURY, NEPTUNE, ATTENDANT TRITONS.

SCENA.

The white cliffs of Albion—Hymeneal Temple in the background—Albion enthroned; Neptune and attendant Tritons grouped at base—The distant Sea with Fleet in view—Mercury in the foreground habited as the "Times."

ALBION—*(gazing over the cliff).*

Come hither, Mercury, what's this I see ?
A gallant fleet comes riding o'er the sea ;
Behold their white sails flutt'ring as they leave
The snowy foam, behind they swiftly leave
    Yon Danish shores.

MERCURY.

    They bring to our proud land
A youthful princess, to bestow her hand
On England's heir, an argosy of bliss,
Old Neptune ne'er bore greater wealth than this.

              (Retires.)

ALBION *(to Neptune).*

Hail ! " Ancient Mariner," becalm thy wave,
Thy Tritons greet the beautiful and brave !

   Tritons prostrate themselves—Distant boom of cannon.

Our sisters linger not, they hither come
To welcome Alexandra to her home :

    * Originally published in the " Curtain," Prince of Wales' Theatre, Liverpool.

See " Cambria" with them, on her maiden-brow
Young Albert's emblem, in fine *feather* now.

Enter Caledonia, Erin, and Cambria.

Go, Neptune, with thy chariot skim the seas,
And fan the ripples with propitious breeze!

Exeunt Neptune with Tritons.

CALEDONIA, ERIN, AND CAMBRIA *(sing)*.

We come, we come,
From our mountains, rivers, vales,
To welcome home
The bride of the " Prince of Wales !"
We bring, we bring,
Hope's garlands to entwine
With wedding ring,
Two fond hearts to combine,
For aye, for aye !

Chorus—all take hands.

Then happiness, bright happiness impart
Its gentle charm o'er every loving heart !
For royal loves we joy foretell.
Whilst pealing anthems upward swell !
Hail ! all hail !

ALBION—*(spoken)*.

Sisters, e'en now the vessels near the strand,
Kissing, as 'twere, our happy, favor'd land—
Behold, they reach the altar, and that vow
Of life-long love are registering now !

*Distant music and bells—the boom of cannon. Albion,
Erin, Caledonia, kneel looking towards the temple.*

CALEDONIA—*(all rising)*.

From Scotia's clime her proud and snow-capped hills—
Her pleasant isles, and dashing mountain rills,
Romantic spots, where ev'ry traveller turns
To dwell on reminiscences of " Burns,"
" Wallace" and " Scott," " The Bruce," and each proud
    name,
Inscrib'd upon th' eternal page of fame,
I bring a welcome from the " plains and fells,"
From all those "moors red-brown wi' heather bells,"
Congratulations ; (there the playful feet
Of Scottish maidens now in dances meet)—
From **our** blest Queen's secluded highland home,
From " banks an' braes," from " dens an' dells" I **come,**
For " Auld lang syne," our Prince, we welcome thee
And " Alexandra" to our " ain countrie !"

ERIN.

" I saw from **the** beach, **when the** morning was shining,
  A bark o'er the waters move gloriously on,"
(Thus wrote **our** " Tom Moore"), and methought, **as**
    reclining,
  I heard his sweet words, but the poet had gone.
Then I rose, **and** cross'd over the seas us dividing,
  And left *my* " green isle," to give joy **in** *your own,*
And **a thought** then came o'er me, that whate'er betiding,
  We love our dear Queen and we honour her throne.
Thus pray'rs pure and holy we raise, **as** returning
  From heaven they hallow **our** Albert's blest name,
That his soul e'er the base **and** unworthy be spurning,
  And give " out its sweets **to Love's** exquisite flame !"

May the halo of " Albert the Great" with him be !
" Alexandra" mavourneen, a welcome to thee !

CAMBRIA.

Since *our* first Edward, in Carnarvon's tow'rs,
Derived by right of birth his princely pow'rs,
Our little princedom, last, not least, in fame,
Hath borne the royal arms and royal name ;
Joy runs throughout her verdant hills and vales,—
Nurseries of strange and legendary tales,—
Tho' small her region, she"ll a *haven* prove
To mighty ships, that now the ocean rove ;
On commerce' page she yet may be so great
As to be no mean pillar of your state.
O happy hour, when Prince of hers doth play
The part of bridegroom in the rites to-day.

ALBION.

E'en so, then, sisters, we'll to Windsor, there
The wedding banquet bid them quick prepare,
For our blest Queen, her regal court adorn,
That she may honour her dear eldest-born !
Come, Mercury, out with all your budget—news—
Ho ! newsboy, letter-bags, newspapers,—lose
No time, we wait—

(Horn outside—Enter Mercury as Post-boy.)

MERCURY.

Here, ladies, is the last,
A precious bit ; Hymen has forged them fast
In *bonds* that never will be out of date,—
And tho' the telegram was rather late,

In every *hamlet* (I don't mean the Dane)
Is lit up quite a " feu de joie," a flame
That, indicative of th' event (" old joke !")
Burns far too brightly e'er to *end in smoke.*
See all my papers, for this blest day dated,
Have caught the blaze, and are *illuminated !*
As on the **ear** the boom of *cannon* falls
The nation threads the giddy *round* of *balls*
And as the news each *column* gladly tells,
Columns of Volunteers (w)ring hands of bell(e)s !
Steel glitters in the sunlight.   Hark ! they come !
        (*Military music without—Wedding March.*)
Put wind in trumpet, *steam* in *kettle*-drum !

                    ALBION.

Then Erin, Caledonia, Cambria, kneel—
That we the glorious Future may reveal !

                        (*They Kneel.*)

Scene opens—discovering " *Albert and Alexandra*" *before
   the altar.   Attendants grouped around.   Cupids
   above.*

                    ALL.

        Our youthful pair now bless,
        And grant them happiness :
            This be our pray'r !
        Now their bright hopes are seal'd,
        Be Thou their gracious shield,
        And heavenly blessings yield
            The bridal pair !

        ————

        GOD SAVE THE QUEEN !

Welcome, Alexandra!

———

Welcome, welcome, Alexandra!
  Welcome to our sea-girt shore ;
Blest the breezes that have fann'd ye
  Hither, to leave us no more!

Brightly sparkling in the sunlight,
  Was each dancing wave that brought
Denmark's ships with such a fair freight,
  Bride our prince hath fondly sought!

Strangely, perhaps, e'en now thou feelest,
  In a land yet strange to thee,
But as thou each wish revealest,
  Thou shalt have sweet sympathy!

Gently strewing round thee flow'rs,
  Are our bright-eyed maidens gay ;
Thus may Fortune deck thine hours—
  May'st thou ever bless to-day!

Florence Nightingale.*

Who watch'd in silent sympathy,
'Midst the sons of victory ?
Who wash'd the festering sore,
'Mid stifled cries and gore,
And nurs'd the stricken sufferer tenderly ?

Who breath'd sweet consolation there,
And bade the gasping brave prepare
For Heaven ?   Was her effort blest ?
He sank **so** gently—to his rest ;
In her bright presence what could he not **bear ?**

Who soften'd down his couch **of pain,**
And did not soften it in vain ?—
Heralded his **soul** to Heaven,
Where the sinner is forgiven,
Where the true warrior meets his truest gain ?

Who spoke to him of native land,
Pressed the Bible in his hand,
Pointed to that blissful shore
Where the soldier toils no more,
And gave his sinking faith **a** helping hand ?

Ye millions, bless her youthful **name !**
To her your gratitude ! **She came**

*Originally published in Eddowes' " Shrewsbury Journal."

From plenty's fav'ring lap to brave
Disease, privation, and the grave,
Her bosom lit with pure and generous flame.

O'er every British hill and vale
May household words e'er breathe the tale
Of philanthropic love,
Thrice hallowed from above,
That fills the heart of Florence Nightingale!

Scenes of the Past.

Scenes of the past,
Too bright to last,
Why should sad memory recall
Back to my mind
That once resign'd ;
Alas ! bid long adieu to all !

Visions of home
(How quickly flown,)
When I was happy 'mid the throng,
Dark clouds float o'er—
I see no more,
Those visions bright fade with my song !

To an Infant.*

Rock on! dear infant; slumber steals
  Around thy cradled form,
And nought to thee as yet reveals
  The sunshine or the storm.
May'st thou, when tossing on life's sea,
As innocent and happy be!

Rock on! to that sweet carol-strain
  Pour'd forth above thy head,
(O mother, breathe it once again
  Beside the infant bed),
Thou know'st how much thou art blest,
While music heralds thee to rest!

Rock on **! no dreams** thy slumbers break,
  'Tis one serene, **soft bliss ;**
Tell **me,** oh Heaven! can language speak
  Of brighter scene than this ?
Ah no ! **and** poetry lacks pow'r
To paint thee, babe, in such an hour.

Rock on ! the troubled world **around**
  Not yet hath claim'd her **son,**
Nor the faint echo of a sound
  Disturb'd thee, little one !
Then take thy rest: care's cruel smart
Too soon shall pain thy spotless heart.
     God bless thee, little one !

*Originally published in the London " Looker On."

The Shepherd's Reply.

The sun had sunk, and left a ray,
That, lingering, shewed his western way
And mellowed glory o'er the floods,
Poured fading streaks, and tinted woods
Swayed gently, as the wind arose,
And tired nature sought repose.

"**Upon** the hill he turned," for there reclined
A youth of rustic habit, but whose mind
Was stored with genial truths and ready wit,
As good as e'er **renowned Joe** Miller writ.
With mien so gentle, his expressive eye
Seemed looking upward to the bright blue sky,
And all his flocks were nibbling pleasure round—
Browsing sweet herbage, dotted o'er the ground.

Lo! where a **satin robe upon the** green
And mossy turf flings **o'er the lovely** scene
A deeper interest, **and** amid **the flowers**
A fair one reads away her cloudless **hours;**
Loving with Petrarch—then anon she fears
With Dante, and with Lamartine sheds tears:
How pleasant 'tis to watch her laughing smile,
As contemplating comic scenes awhile—
Lo! all the passions **of a life-long** book
Are concentrated in **that charming look.**

The volume closed, upraised her eyes,
  She saw the rustic boy ;
Then from the sward did quickly rise,
  And seized with sudden joy,
She looked around with conscious pride ;
  The whole domain to roam
Was hers ; afar she then espied
  Her fine old feudal home,
And gaily to the Shepherd said :—
  " Young man, why don't you play
" Upon your pipe ?" He turned his head,
  And thus to her did say :—

" What, with this ?" ('twas a black 'un—thus he spoke it,)—
"If I've no 'bacca, Marm, how can I smoke it ?"

(*The lady fainted.*)

William Makepeace Thackeray.

Alas, Pendennis ! Thus another star
Hath sunk behind the horizon afar,
Where, one by one, beneath the swollen sea
Of history's past our great have ceased to be.
  Alas ! kind Newcomes, hath relentless death
Seal'd up thy brain, and suck'd **thy gen'rous breath,**
Crush'd thy **gay pen,** bedew'd the world with **tears,**
And closed the **golden volume** of bright **years** ?
  Alas ! 'tis sadly **true, we fondly** weep ;
The Prince of Satire hath lain down in sleep,
And doth not **rise again !**

              Behold that face,
Calm with **a** peaceful triumph, beaming grace—
And past the chisell'd art of mortal hand—
Smiling **farewell** to Vanity-Fair-land !
There **Truth, enthroned, hath** torn the **mask from sin,**
And gazed upon deformity within ;
Here the last satire on life's **motley page,**
In life or death the glory of our age !
    With festive garland weave sad *immortelle,*
    As Epicedian anthems heavenward swell—
    Yield the last tribute to the sterling name
    Of one who slumb'reth in **the lap** of Fame !

Oh, Rest Thee Now, my Own Love!

Oh, rest thee now, my own love,
   For soon in some lone hour
Some sadness may have thrown, love,
   A shadow o'er thy bower!
Sleep, 'ere that maiden-bloom, love,
   Now mantling o'er thy brow,
May pale 'neath ev'ning's gloom, love,
   Or perhaps the broken vow!

Thus, while the green boughs twine, love,
   And lace thy sylvan screen,
A fairy temple's thine, love,
   For fancy's girlish dream,—
O'er all the warm sun-light, love,
   Decks sparkling gems for thee;
Thou'rt young, the sky is bright, love,
   Then sleep, but dream of—me!

The Vesper Bell.*

Hark ! 'tis the sound of " Vespers" o'er the wide
And glassy bosom of the sleeping lake,
The sun's last ling'ring radiance thrown upon
Its gilded margin speaks the approach of night,
And sultry day's decline.   A note swells on
The list'ning ear in soothing melody,
And wraps the soul in deep and sweet devotion.
Yon boatman doth upon his dripping oar
Pause to breathe forth his evening orison ;
With pious awe his form is bent in prayer,
His eyes are raised above, his face attests
That heart and soul are gently raised to Heaven !
Thus all is still, a solemn silence hangs
O'er all, as with the daily welcome voice
Of sacred bell, they give their thoughts to God,
And dedicate their souls to Him alone !

* Originally published in the " Midland Magazine."

Love Treasures.

'Tis a **sweet** voice I hear, breaking softly thro' **trees**
   Brightly tinted by sunlight and show'r,
Their leaves gently sway'd to and fro by the breeze—
   Their boughs twine my wife's charming bow'r.
Thus **she,** resting, reclines, and her little ones round
   Laugh and chatter in innocent glee ;—
A bright solar star, with her starlets around,
   That shine, and shine only for me !

From the furnace-like world, then, so live we, and love,
   Tho' 'tis seething **with** passion and pain,
It seems far away—'midst bird-music and love,
   It may cast us allurements in vain.
And **so** may we live, to our life's utmost length ;
   And **when we** are ancient and grey,
May those children have grown up in goodness and
      strength,
   That are butterfly-hunting **to-day.**

This Heart doth Pine!*

This heart doth pine for thee, my love,
   When thou art far from me ;
Whilst doubting fear and **sadness prove,**
   It throbs alone for thee.
My soul's pure love is all thine own,
    'Tis pledg'd in truth to thee ;
And hope's **sweet solace hath** not flown,
   It still shall comfort **me.**

Then, as the flow'rs await the smile
   Of summer ere they bloom,
I'll stay thy coming, and the while
   Wish that gladcoming soon ;
Or as before the sunshine clear,
   The **show'rs in April** flee,
I'll check the sigh, **and dry the tear,**
   For thou mine **own** wilt be !

* Published by Messrs. Hime and Son, the Music composed
by **J. B. Cooper,** Esq., Liverpool.

A Mother's Love.

How blest the **name of mother !**   Most of **us**
Have felt her tenderness in youth and age ;—
Each of us, like some gently opening flower,
Expanded 'neath her kind congenial smile,
And smiled again in happy innocence.
How often have we, on a winter's night,
When storms swept rudely past, and pelting rain
Dashed o'er our dwelling, with our breathing hushed
Heard with mute wonder and delight the tale
She whispered : for no artificial charm
Adorned her simple story, fancy wrought
No woven wreath of unreality !
How have we hung around her neck, and gazed
Into her eyes **for** comfort, hope, **and** love,
And with our little fingers toyed, and wooed
Her soft and silken hair to twine with ours !
And when, with long years laden, snow-white hair
Her calm brow silvers with serene old age,
We love her, for with ever pious care
She's watched **her** loved ones all rise up around
To bless her fondest hope.
                              She taught **us** truth,
And **bade us love the** good and beautiful ;—
To her the sky breathed silent eloquence,
Each moment great with thought, each twinkling star
A lesson bright to sad mortality !
She told us in her earnest love that these

Were salutary hours **that virtue gives,**
To improve the uncertain tenor of our way—
To fit us for the world, yet still retain
Our faith's allegiance to indulgent Heaven !

Tale-telling,

When little boys and girls will tell
Their little foolish tales, 'tis well
To take a birch and castigate—
'Twill cure them, or at any rate
Th' effect will last until the smart
Has ceased to act upon the heart,
Which if renewed, and often so
The smart increasing with the blow,
'Twill in the end the victory gain,
And will not have been done in vain !

But when big baby-boys relate
To some one else's silly pate
Their childish tricks, and think that gag
Which makes their busy long tongues wag—
Is just the thing to please their friends,
And by soft prattle gain their ends :—
They are beneath the notice quite
Of folk of sense, and 't serves them right,
When from our company they're scouted,
And all their fond conceits well flouted ;
For by society's best rules,
They're class'd with magpies or with fools !

The Contrast.

A whirl—then a dust—'twas the great man pass'd by,
In his chariot with fast coursers curvetting high,
And the poor man hath humbly and abjectly bowed
From the 'midst of the pressing and wondering **crowd,**
To wealth in its panoply !

The poor man is happy, though scanty his store,
He seeketh not alms at the great one's door ;
But his wasting form, and the shrill piping note
That issues from out of his shrively throat,
Can now repine **no more** !

Then **the poor man** dieth, **and no** sculptured stone
Tells of the sigh, and **the** half-stifled **moan**—
Of the low-breath'd murmur and palsied prayer
That the suffering bosom was echoing where
He'd watch'd for his last long home !

Tread softly—the sons of mortality sleep
In their deathly slumber **so darkly and** deep ;—
The great may leave glory behind him, the poor
A name blest in memory that **will endure**
Whilst good men their vigils keep !

* Originally published in the " Midland Magazine."

On the Severn.*

Oh   give me a scene on Sabrina's stream,
  And waft me along her clear water ;
Oh ! give me a dream of that which hath been,
  In days of bold knighthood and slaughter !

When those banks by the flood were bedabbled in blood,
  And the heart of the warrior was fainting,
The Welsh minstrel stood, with his harp and his hood,
  And in verse the wild picture was painting.

Hurrah ! for our bands, as they rode through the lands
  Of the border, where beauty was lending
New strength to their hands, as they fought on the sands
  Of fair Severn, so serpent-like wending !

But 'tis past, long since fled, and those heroes are dead,
  In death alike cruel and gory ;
No tear that was shed for the victims who bled
  Has wash'd out their crimes or their glory !

Oh ! give me a scene on Sabrina's stream,
  And waft me along her clear water ;
I'll care not, I ween, for that which hath been
  In days of bold knighthood and slaughter !

* Originally published in **Eddowes's** *Shrewsbury Journal.*

My dear Old Home.

As the brilliant star
That beams afar,
And tints the darkening hills with light,
E'en so those scenes,
In memory's dreams,
Still rise before us in the night ;
Visions of home
In dreams will come—
In happy dreams, my dear old home !

As the gladdening rays
Of summer days
Are cast athwart the forest shade,
And flowers' bright bloom
Comes with perfume,
O'er the blushing cheek of the forest maid,
So scenes of home
In dreams will come—
In happy dreams, my dear old home !

The Dying Girl.*

Upon a rude and time-worn bed
   A beauteous maiden lay,
For time had fail'd, though it had sped,
   To steal her charms away ;
Soft pillow'd, in a slight repose reclining,
In dire disease she seem'd not slowly pining !

An anxious mother o'er her bent,
   And oft would kneel and pray,
As some kind pitying angel sent
   From heaven to soothe her way ;
She whispered, " Mother, why so often grieving
That this poor soul a sinful world is leaving ?"

But time passed on—one silent night
   There fell upon the ear
A solemn knell that told her flight
   To yon celestial sphere ;
A mother's lips the clay-cold cheek were pressing,
That lay unconscious of the fond caressing !

* Originally published in " Eddowes's Shrewsbury Journal."

All else may Change.

All else may change, and years may fly,
  The sands of life run on,
This heart of mine will e'er be nigh,
  Though time and friends have gone.
My prayer before Love's shrine shall be,
  Content and gladness thine,
And all my spirit's hope shall be
  To make thy gladness mine!

So when our fondest hopes are crown'd
  By life-long earnest bliss,
In one close link our souls are bound
  By love's enduring kiss;
The waves of life may rudely **rise**,
  False friends may **quickly flee**,
Then will I gaze into thine eyes,
  And there my comfort be!

The Four Jolly Smiths.*

Four jolly, jolly smiths, with their hammers great,
  Strike boldly the whole day long;
Each mighty, mighty swing, both early and late,
  Keeps time to a jovial song;
    And the deep-toned note,
    As each hand hath smote,

* Originally published in the *Sheffield Daily Telegraph*.

Is heard loud above the blow ;
　　And the sparks of light,
　　As they gleam so bright,
O'er their swarthy faces glow,
With a bang and a clang, and **a** ring ding dong,
The work goes merrily rolling along.

These jolly, jolly smiths are big, burly boys,
　And their blows fall lustily ;
They jingle, **jingle huge bars, as** lads do toys,
　And dry jokes crack huskily.
　　So with headlong swing,
　　And rebounding ring,
　They tell of good labour done,
　　And each honest name
　　Hath the sterling fame
　These four jolly smiths have won !
With a bang and a clang, **and a ring ding** dong,
The work goes merrily rolling along.

These jolly, jolly smiths, **when** their **hairs turn gray,**
　Will gladly sit down and rest ;
And jollily, **jollily, each one will say,**
　" We have done our very best."
　　Then the thought so dear,
　　Will each bosom cheer,
　That the *young* smiths still strike on,
　　And feed well **the fires**
　　Of their resting sires,
　Who their work have nobly done !
With a bang and a clang, and a ring ding dong,
The work goes merrily rolling along.

The Little Back Parlour.

Come in, come in—from the wintry **wind**,
  And warm your freezing toes ;
Here's a bright fire and faces kind,
  And news how **the world** goes.

Come in, come in—for here **sits mine host**,
  His honest heart is light,
And the song and laugh, and welcome toast,
  Fill up the jovial night.

Come in, come in—and just cast your eye
  On our glorious Boniface,
As he quietly moistens when dry
  His clay with primeval grace.

Come in, come in—just to hear his joke,
  And his hale, youth-giving shout
Of laughter, as he upcurls the smoke
  And bandies the fun about.

Come in, come in—hear the racy joke,
  And relish the merry grin ;
Old stagers fun at each other poke,
  And the witlings wag your fin.

Come in, come in—here's the legal "**rex**,"
  Who says quiet things and **dry** ;—
On the tip of his nose he pops his specs,
  And winks with the " naked eye."

Come in, come in—here's the plaintive youth,
  Who sighs o'er his loved one's name,
With lisp on lip, in his bosom truth,
  For " she lovth him thtill the thame !"

Come in, come in—here's the rattling blade
  Scattering, clattering on ;
In camp, on steed, in pleasure, or trade,
  He chafes and patters along.

Come in, come in—for here's Mister Chub,
  With jolly belly and round :
He puffs and blows when he's snug in " pub,"
  And he loves the puffy sound.

Come in, come in—here's an antique mug,
  One of the olden time,
A pattern card for many a jug
  In ancient pantomime.

Come in, come in—for a sterling heart
  Hath he, and it is sincere ;
He speaks no flattery, plays no part,
  For 'tis simple nature here.

Come in, come in—hear that eloquent throat—
  The broth of a boy admire ;
He'll soon burn holes in the tail of your coat
  With his " raal" Hibernian fire

Come in, come in—for the shades of the great
   Look down from the pictured wall,
And small critics sit in mightier state,
   Their memory to recall!

Come in, then, for often a pleasant look,
   And converse cheerful and gay,
May perhaps wipe a blot from the chequer'd book
   Of life as 'tis passing away!

Oh! 'tis a Pleasant Hour to Me!

Dear lady mine, the bright moonbeams
   Are slowly silvering o'er the sky;
Oh! 'tis the hour when love's soft dreams
   Are gently whispering, thou art nigh.
Oh! 'tis a pleasant hour to me,
When I can dream of love and thee!

Dear lady mine, those orbs of light
   Seem kindling 'neath thy own dear smile,
That perhaps now greets their welcome sight,
   As here I sigh alone awhile.
Oh! 'tis a pleasant hour to me,
When I can dream of love and thee!

PAWSON AND BRAILSFORD, PRINTERS, HIGH-STREET, SHEFFIELD.

www.ingramcontent.com/pod-product-compliance
Lightning Source LLC
Chambersburg PA
CBHW032358020726
47499CB00008B/2799